Edgar & Ellen

RARE BEASTS

Edgar & Ellen

RARE BEASTS

by
CHARLES OGDEN

illustrations by
RICK CARTON

SIMON AND SCHUSTER

First published in Great Britain by Simon & Schuster UK Ltd, 2004,
a CBS Company.

Originally published in 2003 by Tricycle Press, a little division of Ten Speed Press,
P.O. Box 7123, Berkeley, California 94707.

This paperback edition published in 2008 by Simon & Schuster, UK

Design by Star Farm Productions, Inc.
Text and copyright © 2003 by Star Farm Productions Inc.

1 3 5 7 9 10 8 6 4 2

Simon & Schuster UK Ltd
Africa House
64–78 Kingsway
London WC2B 6AH

A CIP catalogue record for this book is available from the British Library.

ISBN: 978-1-84738-279-5

Printed and bound in Great Britain by
CPI Cox & Wyman, Reading, RG1 8EX

WWW.EDGARANDELLEN.COM

Here is my dedication—

to *Rick,* for seeding all those trees years ago
(I chopped them down for firewood),

to *Sara,* for sending me long johns
to wear on the coldest days,

to *Kat,* for humming,

to *Trish,* for making sure I ate breakfast.

Sorry about those cuckoo wasps.

—Charles

It Begins...

The warm night air had a weight to it and hung over the town like a dirty wet dishcloth. It was very late, well past midnight, and the only sounds were the steady chirping of crickets and the occasional hooting of owls.

Down by the river, two shadowy figures danced across the roof of a covered bridge. Flailing their arms and legs about to keep their balance on the steep pitch, they formed whirling silhouettes against the night sky.

"Watch *out,* Sister, you're getting it all over me!"

"Well, if you had remembered a flashlight I'd be able to see what I was doing, Brother."

"Oh, you can see as well as me. You're doing it on purpose."

"Oops!" said Ellen as she dragged her brush across Edgar's face.

"You'll be sorry you did that," he muttered, red paint dripping from the tip of his chin.

"Hush, I'm almost done."

Ellen finished the last letter, and stood back to make sure she had spelled everything properly.

"You forgot the exclamation point!" said Edgar as he dumped what was left in the paint can over his sister's head.

Edgar and Ellen tackled each other and tumbled off the roof, splashing into the water below. Standing in the waist-high river, soaking wet, with red paint flowing as if they were bleeding from terrible wounds, the twins admired their work.

"I like it, Brother."

"It's certainly better than it was before, Sister."

They cackled over the sounds of crickets and owls and crept home.

1. Welcome to Nod's Limbs, Friend

For the most part, Nod's Limbs was a lovely place to live. It wasn't a big town, but it wasn't small either. It was, quite simply, an upstanding community of historic landmarks and charming shopping malls. The Running River cut through the centre of town, although it really should have been called the Walking Stream or the Crawling Trickle since it wasn't very wide and didn't flow very fast. Seven covered bridges allowed people and cars to cross the river, and the townspeople were very proud of their covered bridges. It's rare to see *one* covered bridge in a town these days, and Nod's Limbs had *seven*. They looked like big red barns spanning the river, identical except for what was painted on their roofs.

Each had two words painted in big white block letters, one word on each side. If you were traveling the length of Florence Boulevard, each bridge added another word to a message, and the message was different depending on which direction you were traveling. From east to west, the roofs read "WELCOME FRIEND TO NOD'S LIMBS STAY AWHILE." From west to east they said "COME BACK SOON FRIEND AND TAKE CARE." However, since you could enter Nod's Limbs from the west as easily as from the east, and leave in either direction as well, sometimes these messages made sense and sometimes they didn't. But though you might be wished "WELCOME" as you left and greeted with "COME BACK SOON" as you entered, the residents of Nod's Limbs didn't mind because they thought it looked quaint.

But no matter how respectable a town is, when it's large enough, it usually develops what the locals call the "right side of town" and the "wrong side of town."

The "right side of town" is where the honest, hardworking citizens live. The streets are clean, the lawns are manicured, and people walk around with smiles on their faces and a kind word for their neighbours. On the "wrong side of town," however, people don't look each other in the eye when passing in the street. It's where the disreputable people live, such as those who would deface public property – those who would take the sweet greetings of their town and alter them to say mean things like "WELCOME FIENDS TO SMELLY NOD'S LIMBS DON'T FEED THE ANIMALS" and "DON'T COME BACK HERE EVER EVER EVER." The streets here are covered in trash and dirt, and the houses are dark, dilapidated, and terribly unpleasant.

Nod's Limbs was large enough to have a "right side" and a "wrong side," and you might think that both "sides" of the town would be about the same size. Not so in Nod's Limbs.

"An honest day's work for an honest day's pay" was the credo of most of the town's citizens, and because of this dedication, just about the whole of Nod's Limbs could be considered the "right side."

All, that is, except for one small block on the far end of town.

2. The Wrong Side

If you walked south through Nod's Limbs, past the parks and trees and row after row of well-kept houses, past the zoo and the high school and the hospital, and finally past the solemn green hills of the Nod's Limbs Cemetery, you'd come to Ricketts Road.

Ricketts Road ran along the edge of the Black Tree Forest Preserve from the east end of town to the west. It was a charming two-lane road, and the Nod's Limbs Maintenance Department did an admirable job of keeping the pavement clean and the roadside vegetation trimmed.

However, just past where the back of the cemetery met Ricketts Road, there was a turnoff for a narrow little lane that was never touched by the Maintenance Department. The lane had no name, or at least no street sign, and it was badly in need of a new layer of tar. The broken, weed-choked pavement made walking hazardous and driving treacherous, so it was very rarely travelled.

The lane came to a dead end in front of a very tall, very narrow house that rose so far into the sky that you could fall over backwards trying to see the top of it. Two high arched windows gave the impression that the imposing structure was watching you, and above them the house was capped with a dark cupola with wrought-iron spikes reaching skywards and a small round window in the centre that looked like a mystical third eye.

And the colour! Or, more to the point, the lack of colour! There was one word for this place, and that was *grey*. Everything on the house was some shade of grey, from the bottommost stones to the tips of the spikes jutting up from the roof. The worn wood trim on the doors and windows was such a deep and heavy grey that it was almost black, and the slate shingles looked like the

inside of an abandoned furnace. A few broken shutters dangled from their hinges, swaying back and forth, caught in the wind that gusted continually about the tall building.

And if you came close to the house, right up to the front steps, you'd be able to read the one strange word carved in stone above the door. In neat, chiselled letters, such as those you might find on a gravestone, it said:

A funny-sounding word with a rather unfunny meaning, *schadenfreude* means "pleasure derived from the misery of others," and it was a fitting motto for those who lived there.

And, perhaps, it served as a warning for curious passers-by, as well.

3. The Twins

Looming over the landscape and casting a long shadow, this mansion rarely drew anyone close enough to read the word carved above the door. The house was so ornate and eye-catching that it might have been beautiful had someone *else* lived there. Had someone *else* lived there, with a fresh coat of paint and a petunia border around the lawn, it might have been bright and welcoming and the most popular house in town.

Alas, someone else did not live there. *Two* some-one elses lived there: Edgar and his sister Ellen. These two were not just brother and sister – they were twins, and should just one of them be trouble, then two most certainly would be double that. And just one was very troublesome indeed.

> *"The garden's growing high, Sister."*
> *"Time to tear the petals off the roses, Brother!"*

The twins were tall and scrawny, with black hair matted flat to their heads. Ellen's limp pigtails dangled past her pointy chin, while Edgar's hair was all one short length, except for the few strands that stuck

straight up in the back. Both had pale, angular faces and wide, bulging eyes.

They wore matching one-piece, striped footie pyjamas, with flaps on the seat that were handy when they needed to use the lavatory. The old, worn-in pyjamas were very comfortable, and the twins kept them on all the time. What were once red and white stripes were now a stained and dingy rust and grey.

Their skills in the art of mischief were impressive and long-studied, having begun twelve years earlier in the womb. Although they were twins, Ellen was technically older by two minutes and thirteen seconds.

Oh, the fight the two of them put up to see who would enter the world first!

Their mother suffered hours upon hours of pain in the hospital delivery room as they punched and kicked each other inside her. Ellen must have edged out Edgar, because she finally emerged first, miniature fists held high in victory celebration. Edgar came soon after, and when the nurses first held up the twins side-by-side for their mother and father to see, Edgar took his tiny finger and poked Ellen in the eye.

4. Hide-and-Seek

One day near the end of summer, Ellen examined her garden through a grimy window and saw that it was wilting nicely in the muggy, late-morning heat. She hadn't watered any of the plants or fed the fanged orchids in weeks, and the foliage had a pleasing droop, as if the plants might reach the ground and try to crawl toward nourishment and shelter. There was no need for Ellen to go out, as she had planned, to prune the hemlocks. So while most of Nod's Limbs' younger citizens were splashing in pools or frolicking by the river, Edgar and Ellen stayed inside their dark house, playing a game of hide-and-seek.

The twins' home had many floors including a subbasement, a basement, an attic, and an attic-above-the-attic. Although the house was so narrow that each floor had only two or three rooms, there were still an awful lot of them. Each room was full of cupboards and closets and couches and curtains, and enough grubby cubbyholes to hide in for an entire summer's worth of hide-and-seek.

Edgar and Ellen's parents had long since departed on an extended "around the world" holiday. At least that's what it said on the note they'd left behind. With no one to clean it, the vast house had accumulated a rich collection of cobwebs and dust balls, providing the perfect setting for their game, to which they added their own unique twist.

In a typical game of hide-and-seek, the game ends once one player discovers where another is hiding. Well, Edgar and Ellen's version didn't end by merely *finding* the hider. The game ended when the hider was *subdued,* which meant that the seeker first had to uncover the hiding place and then had to wrestle the hider to the ground. Subduing could be quite a struggle since the twins knew each other's wrestling moves, and the game generally concluded with either the hider or the seeker bound hand and foot, tied up in the ropes they both routinely carried.

Of course, once one twin was trussed up, he or she had lost and was at the mercy of the winner, and the winner always made sure to show as little mercy as possible before darting off to find a new hiding spot, leaving the loser to struggle free.

Ellen was adept at using her teeth and sharply filed nails to cut through her bonds, and Edgar had practiced the deliberate methods of famous escape artists. Nevertheless, it usually took each sibling over an hour to work free of the ropes. And an hour is plenty of time to find a great hiding place.

5. A Need for Something New

Ellen was in the library, wedged into a shallow compartment behind an ugly oil painting – a rotting still life of mouldy cabbage and eggs. She felt cramped and restless in the tiny alcove.

"What's taking Edgar so long?" she thought, wondering why she couldn't have picked a larger hiding place. "Curse that slow brother of mine, always checking every possible spot on every floor, even ones we've already used!"

Suddenly, she heard the sombre tones of the house's pipe organ waft up from a parlour on the seventh floor. Edgar was playing a military march.

"Argh! Not again!" Ellen wailed, covering her ears.

But Ellen's grimace turned into a smile as she ran her fingers over the edge of the strange item she'd brought with her, a surprise she thought her brother might appreciate.

Finally, the cacophony ended and a slight gust of chilly air tingled the hairs on the back of Ellen's neck. She knew Edgar had entered the library. He had tracked her there after nearly two hours of searching, although he might have arrived sooner had he not run into all the booby traps she had rigged. He had managed to avoid the oil slick on the second-floor landing, but the trip wires laced through the fourth and fifth floors had taken some time to disarm, and a falling bucket in the kitchen had nearly given him a good knock on the head.

Ellen watched from a gap between the frame and the wall as her twin checked behind drapes and under chairs. When Edgar turned to examine a massive mahogany desk, she carefully swung the painting outwards, climbed down to the dusty carpet, and crept up behind him.

"Too slow, Edgar, TOO SLOW!" she screamed as she pounced.

Edgar was unprepared for Ellen's attack, and before he could defend himself, Ellen had him flat on his back atop the desk. She quickly bound him in place and, while Edgar squirmed, she climbed up on the desktop. As she stood above him, Edgar got a good look at what she was holding.

Hanging from one end of a long, golden cord was a sharp, moon-shaped metal blade. Edgar recognized the tool; he had designed it himself to cut down political banners during Nod's Limbs' last elections.

Ellen held the cord over her brother and began to swing it gently.

The sharp metal crescent started to swing as well. Ellen smiled as she let a short bit of cord slip through her fingers, allowing the crescent to descend a few inches.

Edgar watched the blade sweep closer and closer, its arc widening and accelerating with each pass. It looked like the pendulum of a fiendish grandfather clock.

"Tick tock," Ellen said with a yawn. "Tick tock."

"Oh, tick tock, pish posh," grumbled Edgar, as he started working the knots.

Ellen patiently lowered the crescent, and it whistled through the air above her brother. Edgar continued to probe the ropes without a hint of panic.

"Tick tock, Brother…" said Ellen as she let her attention wander. Her wrist was getting a bit sore from swinging.

"Yeah, yeah, drip drop," replied Edgar.

Soon Edgar had loosened his bonds enough to wiggle his fingers, but his focus was also drifting. How many times before had he wriggled out of these ropes?

As the crescent swept so close to Edgar's chest that he could feel a breeze on his face, so close that the ropes that held him frayed and snapped as the metal cut into them, the twins looked each other in the eye.

Ellen looked down at Edgar, and Edgar glared back up at Ellen, and after a long summer hiding, seeking, subduing, wrestling, and booby-trapping, both of them said,

"I'm bored."

6. Possibilities

"We could clog the sewer tunnels with giant pillows," suggested Edgar, when he'd finally freed himself from his bonds. "When it rains, the streets will flood and we can sail around town in a boat. That would be fun!"

"That's too complicated," Ellen replied. "How would we make the pillows? We don't have any money to buy mountains of feathers and fabric, and neither of us knows how to sew, you idiot."

Ellen tugged at her pigtails as she thought. "Hmmm, how about something simple? Let's get big sacks of white pepper and dump them into the batter at Buffy's Muffins!"

Edgar rolled his eyes. "As much as I'd like those goody-goody townspeople to suffer endless sneezing fits, where would we get the pepper, dummy?"

He scratched the tip of his pointy, pale chin.

"Hmmm...we could swipe the wash off old Mrs Haggardly's clothes line and take it to the Laundromat. Run those clothes through the industrial dryer a few times, and they'll shrink to half their size! We'll hang them back up on her line, and when she finds them, she won't know *what* to do!"

"Oh *Edgar,*" chided Ellen. "Do *you* have all the quarters to run the dryer over and over? No, you don't, and neither do I. Besides, we pulled that trick on Mrs Haggardly before, and she didn't even notice. What fun is that?"

The twins stood in the middle of the library, their shoulders hunched as they strained to come up with another idea.

"We need money, Sister," said Edgar. "What can we possibly do for fun without money?"

After a moment of concentration, a grin spread across Ellen's face and she uttered one word in reply:

"Pet!"

7. Pet

Whenever the two children grew tired of annoying and harassing each other and were at a loss for some new nefarious scheme or unsuspecting victim, there was always something else in the house to poke and prod. That something else was Pet.

Pet usually stayed as far out of Edgar and Ellen's way as it could, preferring long lonely days of cowering in the dark to long disturbing days at the mercy of its merciless masters. However, it was now almost noon on Tuesday, and that meant it was time for *Around the World with Professor Paul,* Pet's favourite nature programme.

Knowing Pet's fondness for the Professor, the twins found it in the den, perched upon the back of a dark leather wingback chair, illuminated by the

flickering light of the large black-and-white television.

Pet didn't look like any other kind of animal you've ever seen. It wasn't very large. It didn't have scales or feathers. It was a matted ball of long, dark hair, similar in appearance to an old dirty wig. Pet had no ears, nose, or mouth that could be seen, nor had it visible arms or legs, and the small heap sat so still on the chair that it would be easy to mistake it for an oversized ball of lint. Well, except for the single milky yellow eye that sat atop the tangled pile of hair.

Pet had lived in the house with Edgar and Ellen for as long as they could remember. The twins had first noticed Pet behind a large wooden wine cask in the cellar. Since Pet didn't seem to eat much or make much noise – in fact, they never witnessed Pet doing much of anything – they decided to keep it.

How lucky for Pet.

8. Today's Programme

And so it happened that just as Edgar had finished binding Pet's shaggy body to a long wooden pole, and just as Ellen was about to collect the spiderwebs from the ceiling of the den with their new Pet-broom, Professor Paul announced something on TV that grabbed the siblings' attention:

> *"Today, we're going to explore the amazing world of exotic animals. The rarest of the rare, the most unique of the unique, the cream of the crop, these magnificent creatures are worth their weight in gold.* **These are the most valuable animals on Earth!**
>
> *"Join me, Professor Paul, as we meet wealthy collectors from all over the world who covet these amazing beasts and are willing to*

pay thousands to own one. For the richest of the idle rich, money is no object, and exotic animals make much more fashionable pets than dogs and cats...."

Edgar and Ellen stopped listening. A scheme was forming.

"If we had our own exotic animals to sell," said Edgar, "we'd make enough money to construct giant pillows *and* buy white pepper. We'd have enough to carry out all of our plans!"

"Think BIG, Edgar! If we were rich, rich, *rich,* just *imagine* what we could do," said Ellen. "We wouldn't have to stop with the *small* ideas we've had before.

"If we bought a hang glider and a giant tank of fizzy cola, we could take off from the top of our house and spray all the soccer fields from above. Turn them into sudsy, sticky messes!" she said, twisting her pigtails.

"We could erect a giant windmill, buy tons of manure, and blow the stink all over town." Edgar was bursting with enthusiasm. "P-U, nobody would go outside for days because of the smell! We'd have the toy stores and candy shops and ice cream parlours all to ourselves!"

"We could buy a whole carnival and put the tents right in the middle of town," Ellen said.

"And we could keep the bright coloured lights and music on all night and day, and never let anyone else in to enjoy the games and rides!" added Edgar.

They grinned at each other as they mulled over all these new ideas for mischief and mayhem.

9. Aha!

Edgar and Ellen climbed the steep staircase to the ninth floor. The whole floor was one big open room, and the twins used it as their ballroom when they were in a festive mood. Two large arched windows in the front wall (the ones that looked like watchful eyes from the outside) let in a fair amount of light during the day, making it the least dismal room in the house.

Edgar and Ellen danced and pranced their way across the room, cackling as they went:

> *A plan, a scam, is what we need*
> *To fund our games and revelries.*
> *Our clever minds are guaranteed*

To conjure up some brilliant deeds.
There is no plot we can't concoct,
Our brains, with schemes, are overstocked,
And kids from all around the block
Fear our genius 'round the clock.
Look out, look out! For here we come
To hatch our plans for pranks and fun!

Edgar and Ellen stopped in the centre of the ballroom. Hanging from the ceiling was a rusty iron ring anchored to a trap door. Ellen climbed up onto Edgar's shoulders and pulled it. The trap door swung down with a loud *"creak"* and a worn set of wooden steps unfolded. The two scampered up to the attic.

The twins masterminded their most impressive plots in the attic, and it was easy to see why. Crates and tools and dusty birdcages, mouldy steamer trunks and broken chandeliers, headless mannequins, dented suits of armour, a couple of rusty wrought-iron beds – the attic was piled high with treasures. Picking through the debris usually helped Edgar and Ellen concoct something wicked.

They plunged into the stacks of junk, flinging objects about as they searched for inspiration.

"Aha!" said Ellen, holding up a dented bedpan.

"Oh, come on, Sister, what could we use *that* for?" scoffed Edgar. He emerged from under a ratty tarp, cradling a collection of dirty test tubes and beakers. "Look what I found! Maybe we could run some *experiments*."

Before Ellen could point out that they had nothing to experiment on, she happened to look out of the attic's single round window.

"Brother! Do you see what I see?" she squealed, dropping the bedpan.

Edgar came over to look out the window. "Sister, are you thinking what I'm thinking?" said Edgar. "Come on, let's take a closer look!"

They clambered up one last ladder, tucked away in the back corner. Leading the way, Ellen pushed against the ceiling with her shoulder until another trap door creaked open, and the twins entered the highest room in the house.

Since the attic-above-the-attic provided a remarkable view of the entire neighbourhood, Edgar and Ellen used it as an observatory, and it was barren save for a powerful telescope angled through a slot in the roof. Focusing the lens on the neat, tidy houses and lawns below, they saw a wide variety of dogs lounging in front of doghouses, napping or chewing

on bones. They saw cats walking on fences and climbing trees. They saw bunnies inside their cages sipping from water bottles, and birds basking in the sun on their perches.

"Look at all of those animals," whispered Ellen.

"Right outside our door," answered Edgar.

Deep in thought, the two descended to the attic and paced the floor, leaving tracks in the dust.

They eventually came to a stop by the grimiest corner of the room. Edgar and Ellen contemplated the big mouldy cardboard box that held the hundreds of holiday decorations they'd collected over the years, usually nabbed from an unsuspecting neighbour's front door or the holiday display in the centre of town.

"Glitter and garlands, Brother," Ellen remarked.

"Shiny bulbs and colourful dyes, Sister," added Edgar.

"Very exotic!" they marvelled, arching their eyebrows.

And, just like that, a plan fell into place.

10. Heimertz

Edgar and Ellen chuckled and chortled and whooped. Their new scheme was simple, yet ingenious.

"Brother, I've found something wonderful," Ellen said as she prised open a crate near the box of decorations. Edgar helped wrench off the wooden slats and whispered "Oh!" as he pulled out buckled strips of leather and little wire baskets. The twins put the leashes and muzzles in the box of holiday decorations and dragged it all down to the basement, along with an assortment of dyes, glues, markers, and paints.

Ellen coiled lengths of rope over her left shoulder, and over her right she draped a large gunnysack that held a number of smaller, empty sacks. Edgar grabbed his special dark canvas satchel, which always held a variety of objects. Spoons, saltshakers, bonnets, twine – the items in Edgar's bottomless satchel would seem ordinary to most people, but in his hands they were something, well...*not*. He added the muzzles to the contents. Outfitted with the necessary equipment, brother and sister left their house and skulked across the drab garden, anxiously scanning the gnarled overgrowth for any sign of Heimertz.

Heimertz was the caretaker, tending to the maintenance of the house and grounds, and had worked there for as long as the twins could remember. He always moved slowly, barely flexing his knees as he went, but he had the uncanny ability to appear without warning, emerging silently from the gloom of the house. It disturbed the twins that in one moment they could be playing alone, and in the next find Heimertz and his vacant smile looming over them. *Very* few things unsettled Edgar and Ellen, but Heimertz was one of them.

Whether or not the caretaker actually took any care was debatable, since the house was always dark and sooty and musty, and the garden dense with weeds and roots and dead bushes. But while he made them uneasy, Edgar and Ellen approved of his work – or lack of it.

Heimertz inhabited a bleak shed in a low, swampy

corner of the yard. Marshy mud and reeds rose up high along its ramshackle walls, making the shed look like it was sinking slowly into the earth. There was only one window, and it was cracked and missing a pane of glass. The twins had once peered through, out of curiosity, and inside was but a bare room, simply furnished with a camp bed, a few candles, an old accordion, and a collection of tools, with no other personal effects that might hint at the caretaker's history.

He was rarely seen outside the grounds of the twins' home. Older residents of Nod's Limbs sometimes whispered that, long ago, Heimertz was a Bavarian circus performer who had escaped his family of clowns and acrobats. Edgar and Ellen could never confirm or dismiss the story. The twins found the caretaker too creepy to ask, and even if they could muster up the gumption to speak to him, it was doubtful he would answer. In all these years, Heimertz had never uttered a single word to them.

11. Lurking and Slinking

To their relief on this hot afternoon, the twins could make out Heimertz far off on the other side of the grounds. He was busy ripping large chunks of bark off some decaying trees, so Edgar and Ellen silently crept through their backyard and slipped out into the neighbourhood.

They had to be very sneaky, because Edgar and Ellen had a reputation around town. At one time or another, most children in Nod's Limbs had fallen victim to one of the twins' insidious plots, whether they were aware of it or not. It was not so long ago that the twins had stranded nine-year-old Artie Anderson atop the tallest tree on the block, promising him access to a most amazing tree house. Shortly thereafter they had enticed little Sara Bergstaff to dig for gold in her yard, rupturing her family's septic tank.

So, carefully, very carefully, Edgar and Ellen slid through the shadows. One by one, they visited each house in the neighbourhood. And one by one, they snatched up all the pets.

Some animals were easy to get, since no one was around to keep an eye on them. Their owners were off doing other things, such as buying comic books or playing kickball. Edgar plucked Ronnie Wringwood's dog from in front of its doghouse, and Ellen reached through an open window to nab Heather Redder's parakeet from its cage, leaving nothing but a few fallen feathers.

Other pets required more stealth, and the twins found they needed to create distractions. Edgar pulled popcorn from the depths of his satchel and laid a trail down the driveway of the Bogginer home. While young, peckish Donald Bogginer was lured away by this surprise afternoon snack, Ellen made off with his kitten, Chauncey. Two houses down the street, Ellen rang Franny Finkle's doorbell and then hid behind the family car. When Franny came running to answer the front door ("Coming, Mr Crapple! You better have mail for ME! Mail for *ME!*" she shrieked), Edgar ran around to the back door and grabbed her hamster.

Up one street and down another, the twins added to their collection. They muzzled the surprised pets

to keep them from barking or meowing or making any loud noises, and then stuffed them into the burlap bags. Soon, their collection grew large enough that Edgar and Ellen found it hard to carry, so they set everything down to rest.

"These animals are heavy, Edgar. All their squirming doesn't help, either."

"My arms are starting to get sore, too. But don't worry, Ellen, I've got a plan for transporting our cargo tomorrow. Just you wait!"

"Well, I won't – hey you! Pipe down!" Ellen whispered as a steady low wail came from one of the sacks. Some of the pets began to growl and whine, so the twins poked and prodded the sacks with their toes, trying to keep the animals quiet.

"Noisy things," muttered Edgar. "If we don't watch out, they're going to give us away. We'd better carry these home where no one will hear them, and then we can come back for more!"

The twins lugged the sacks back to their garden, where they piled them in the overgrowth. Returning to their task, they continued down the block, Ellen filching pets and Edgar running the new finds back to their stash.

They came upon a bright yellow house on the

corner, its pretty painted mailbox decorated with bees, butterflies, and the family name *Pickens*. There was an enormous cage in the middle of the back-yard, and coiled in the centre of it, fast asleep, was the largest snake the twins had ever seen. Edgar and Ellen had to take a moment to admire the sheer size of the thing, wrapped around and around itself, forming a snoring pyramid.

It didn't wake up as Ellen opened the cage door and manoeuvred behind it. Edgar held open the biggest sack they had, and his sister grunted as she pushed the massive reptile through the gate of its cage and into the bag. The snake stirred and half opened one eye, but Edgar lifted its tail in his arms and rocked it gently until the snake let out a low whistling snore and returned to its nap.

"That's a full load by itself," Ellen said. "You take it home while I go look for more animals." Edgar shuffled back to their house, huffing and puffing from the weight of the snake. He pushed open the back gate with his foot and staggered into the yard. As the gate swung closed behind him, Edgar stopped suddenly, his breath catching in his throat.

All of the restless sacks were still thrashing about, small sounds emanating from within. And standing above the many bags, leaning over for a closer look, was Heimertz. The stocky caretaker lowered himself to his hands and knees and took great big sniffs of air around the sacks.

Edgar didn't know what to do. The caretaker was inches away from uncovering their ill-gotten booty. A simple tug on one sack's cord was all that was needed. Edgar tried to stand very still but the heavy snake was making his arms ache.

Heimertz sat back on his haunches as the animals, lost in the darkness of the burlap bags, shivered and whined. It seemed an eternity before Heimertz stood, wiping his hands on his stained overalls.

Edgar felt a chill as Heimertz turned and stared at the giant sack in the boy's arms. He inhaled deeply, as if to draw the scent off Edgar and his parcel from across the garden.

Edgar gulped. Without Ellen, he felt particularly vulnerable.

The caretaker's habitual smile twitched; his nostrils flared wide. He stood still for several tense moments, giving no clue as to his next move.

Maybe it heard Edgar's heart pounding furiously, or maybe it felt Heimertz's eerie presence, or possibly it was just having a bad dream, but the snake

stirred against the boy's chest. Edgar, already un-
nerved by the caretaker, let out a jumpy "Eeee-*ah!*"
as he let the sack drop to the ground.

Heimertz briefly surveyed the rest of the grounds
before pivoting his short bulk on his left foot and
stumping off toward the shed.

Edgar fled the garden.

The snake shifted in the burlap and settled back
into deep sleep, resuming its whistling snore.

Edgar caught up with his sister on the far side of
the neighbourhood, huddled in the shadows of a tall
hedge.

"It's Heimertz, Ellen! He caught me with our
stockpile!" Edgar gasped. "He just walked away, but
I didn't know what to do!"

"Hush, Edgar! Hush! I'm trying to be discreet!"

Ellen nodded her head toward the yard beyond
the hedge, and Edgar peeked around it.

Leanne Casey and her friend Bruno were chasing
his miniature dachshund around the grass, laughing
as the wiener dog ran in bigger and bigger circles.
With a playful yelp, the dachshund circled the edge
of the yard, and as he darted behind the hedge, Ellen
lowered her open sack and the dog ran right into it.

By the time Leanne and Bruno rounded the

bushes, there was nothing to see. They stood dumb-founded in the quiet street, listening for a telltale bark, hearing nothing but silence.

And so it went, the twins skulking through the neighbourhood, emerging from the shadows just long enough to snatch a pet before disappearing again. Soon they had amassed a sizable collection of furry, scaly, and feathered creatures, each in its own gunnysack.

Before most of the neighbourhood kids realized that their beloved animals were missing, Edgar and Ellen had dragged the valuable prizes home.

12. Down in the Basement

Pet huddled in a dark corner among the dust balls and cobwebs, safely out of Edgar and Ellen's way, as it watched them haul their spoils through the dusty front hall and pile the sacks by the basement door.

Ellen held the door open.

"After you, Brother."

"No, Sister, after *you!*" Edgar shoved Ellen into the dark stairwell.

With a practiced reflex, she grabbed hold of

Edgar's collar as she toppled. They rolled over each other down the stone steps and landed with a thud. A cold draft blew in from an iron grate in the cement floor.

"Very graceful, Sister."

"Oh, *you're* one to talk."

One by one, the twins shuttled the sacks down from the hall, keeping a wary eye on each other as they passed on the stairs.

When they were finished, Edgar and Ellen huddled in the dank basement over the writhing sacks at their feet. Ellen spread out grubby white sheets stolen from Mrs Haggardly's yard to cover long worktables. Edgar removed the decorations from the battered carton, and, like a surgeon laying out his implements in an operating room, he delicately set all the ribbons and ornaments in a neat row.

"Who might be in here?" Edgar selected a sack and shook out the contents. A kitten tumbled onto the table.

"Oh, you're just a plain little kitty now," he said, removing its muzzle, "but cheer up! Soon you'll be the talk of the town!"

Edgar used paint to change the feline's fur from brown to several shades of blue and purple. He took his time affixing two small twigs to the creature's head and attached a round red ornament to its nose. What was a cat now looked like a glitzy miniature reindeer.

"Hello, little Hamble!" Edgar exclaimed, holding it up so he could look into its mismatched eyes. "Not another one like you in all the world. Definitely exotic! Definitely worth a lot of money!" The Hamble mewed and clawed at its twig antlers.

"Your Hamble isn't nearly as exotic as my Uggpron or these Snifflepops," said Ellen. Edgar turned to see that in the time he'd spent transforming one animal, his sister had placed a grass wreath around a poodle's neck and dyed the whole animal red, turning it into a little crimson lion, and two once-white bunnies were now decked in glitter and feathers.

"We're going to make a fortune!" cheered the twins as they removed the rest of the animals from their sacks. They leashed the creatures to a crusty water pipe so the bewildered menagerie couldn't run away from the fun.

Paint and glue and glitter flew about the basement. The twins gleefully decorated the pets as if they were Easter eggs, singing a little song while they worked.

We've got rare pets, so place your bets
On how much each little critter nets.
People will come on private jets,
Phone their accountants, hire new vets.
So dump more glitter, squirt more glue,
Colour them purple, orange, blue.
Soon they'll be ready for their debut
And we'll rake in the revenue!

Puppies and kitties. Bunnies and birds. Hamsters, gerbils, lizards, and a chicken. Dozens of pets separated from their loving owners, trapped in the dank basement, each undergoing its own unique and terrible transformation.

Oh, the horror!

13. A Little Night Music

It had grown very late by the time Edgar and Ellen completed their exotic collection. The twins would have danced and pranced to celebrate had they not been so tired from a long day of scheming and pilfering and disguising.

They secured the leashes and spread pages of the *Nod's Limbs Gazette* on the floor so things wouldn't get too messy during the night. Then they turned out the basement lights, leaving the animals alone at last, and wearily climbed the many flights of stairs to the attic bedroom.

"Please, no snoring and snorting tonight, Brother," said Ellen as she shuffled across the room.

"Sweet dreams to you, too, Sister," sneered Edgar, as he headed toward his stained pillow and mattress.

As they were about to crawl into their iron-framed beds, they noticed a steady, groaning noise rising up from the world outside. The twins climbed up the ladder to their observatory in the attic-above-the-attic and peered out through the telescope at the neighbourhood below.

It was chaos. Gathered in sad little groups under the streetlights, children cried and screamed and

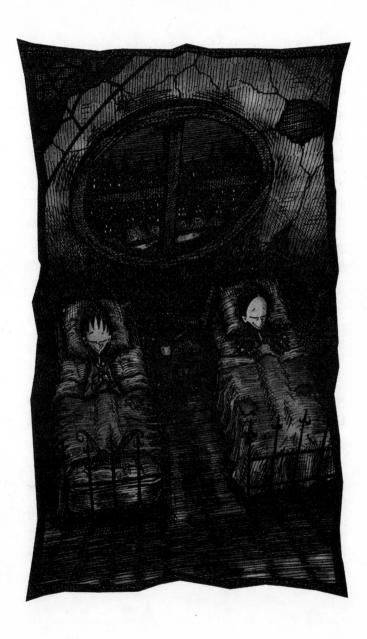

moaned, lamenting the loss of their precious pets. Their parents, unable to enjoy their usual quiet evenings at home with nightcaps and news programmes, were out searching for the missing animals, shouting their names and screaming curses, adding to the din of the children's wails. This tuneless chorus of misery and despair, this sad song of pain and heartache, lasted well into the night.

The echoing lament lulled Edgar and Ellen to sleep, and they slumbered peacefully.

They had a big day ahead of them.

14. The Exotic Animal Emporium

While the rest of the neighbourhood woke to hopelessness and mourning, the likes of which Nod's Limbs had never known, Edgar and Ellen leapt out of bed. Today they were going to get rich!

They abandoned their morning routine of tracking down Pet and roughly scouring its matted hair with their toothbrushes, and instead slid down flight after flight of banisters, cackling all the way to the back door and out into the garden. Strains of accordion music drifted from Heimertz's shed, and they were thankful that the caretaker was occupied.

The twins needed something to transport their magnificent menagerie around town. Edgar led his sister to the centre of the garden, where they cleared away the tangles of witchgrass and knotweed that hid an old, rusted cart. The dry brown stalks and stems poking through the wheels and twisting around the axles made it clear that Heimertz hadn't used it in a long time, if ever, and it took some effort to free the long cart and roll it to a flat patch of dirt.

Edgar and Ellen returned to the attic and grabbed a few large pieces of cardboard and some paint. They also dragged down an old puppet theatre they had stolen the previous year from Mrs Pringle's kindergarten class during nap time. The cloth puppets had long since been chewed apart by rats and moths, leaving nothing but a giant wooden box with a burgundy velvet curtain closed across its stage.

Outside, they hoisted the theatre onto the cart. Edgar took some cardboard and painted a sign that read *"Exotic Animal Emporium,"* and beneath that *"Rare Beasts for Sale,"* and Ellen nailed it to the top of the little theatre.

They found the animals exactly where they had left them in the cold basement, and they carried the wriggling creatures out to the cart. Leashed inside the puppet theatre, smaller animals in front and larger ones in back, they formed an impressive display.

Edgar and Ellen made a sign for each animal listing its species, habitat, price, and a description of its particular origin:

CRACKERMACKER
From the mountains of Dronkle
Only $1,000!
Rescued from the Dronkle City Animal Pound

FREEPLEWINK
From the desert region of Brifftevo
A steal at $2,500!
Traded from an exotic animal dealer for a Splunx

MONDOPILLAR
Terra-aquatic, Uwentic Ocean region
$5,000! Cheap at twice the price!
Captured on a Mondopillar hunt last year

Ellen even gave the animals a little pep talk: "All of you look so much better than you did yesterday. You are incredible creatures now, worth thousands of dollars. And while you may feel a little uncomfortable at the moment, at what price beauty and fame? Anyway, none of this is as bad as that humiliating sweater they made you wear last winter, or all those times they forced you to attend their tea parties."

"Sister, I don't know why you bother."

"Well, you've always been a little slow. When the perky, happy-looking ones sell for more than the asking price, you'll see."

When the animals were hidden behind the closed theatre curtains, their shop-on-wheels had the look of an old-time travelling medicine show.

"Ready to strike it rich, Brother?" Ellen took hold of the front wagon handle.

"Nod's Limbs will be amazed, Sister," replied Edgar as he took up position behind the cart.

With Edgar pushing and Ellen pulling and steering, the cart lurched forward and lumbered unsteadily down the nameless lane and out onto Ricketts Road.

15. Missing!

As Edgar and Ellen rolled their wagon west, they passed coloured pieces of paper taped and tacked to every telephone pole and lamp post. If the twins had paid any attention to the tear-stained, handwritten flyers, they would have seen:

MISSING!

Bain Bean

My German shepherd puppy

Contact Ritchie ASAP!

555-8328

HELP!

I can't find Hodgekiss!

Have you seen my brown bunny rabbit?

—Kyle, 555-9896

LOST!

MY CAT

Answers to the name Blumpers

Mostly black with white feet and a pink nose

Please call Annie at Annie's house, 555-1722

There were dozens of posters in a rainbow of colours, each one crying out for a different missing pet and featuring a crayon drawing or blotchy photograph. Edgar and Ellen rumbled past flyer after flyer, oblivious to all of them, including the one which warned:

16. Open for Business

Edgar and Ellen stopped the cart about a hundred yards down Ricketts Road, where the street intersected with Cairo Avenue, one of several streets in the small town named after much more impressive cities.

Cairo Avenue led north into Nod's Limbs' business district and people on their way to work drove right past the intersection.

"How does this spot look to you, Sister?" Edgar asked.

"Fantastic, Brother," she answered. "Business people make *oodles* of money! I can't wait to get a great big pile of it!"

They pulled back the theatre curtain, revealing the animals. The display looked a bit like a summertime lemonade stand, except instead of pitchers of refreshing lemonade, the twins had expensive and gruesome beasts. The two stood in front of their stand, bellowing like carnival barkers and waving their arms madly.

"Roll up!" yelled Edgar, "Roll right up and witness the marvels of the animal kingdom!"

"Come see for yourselves!" called Ellen, "See what has never been seen before!"

Cars cruised through the intersection, but not one came close to stopping. When too many vehicles passed by for Ellen's liking, she shoved her brother out into the road to block traffic.

A line of cars screeched to a halt in front of the ghastly pale, pyjama-clad boy. The drivers were much more alarmed than Edgar at the possibility of hitting him, but after they established that he was unhurt, they noticed the cart on the side of the road.

Several men and women got out of each car, all of them dressed neatly in business suits. They walked up to the wagon and began looking over the merchandise. A small black poodle shrouded in silver tinsel recognized a family member in the crowd and began to whimper and scratch, but the swarm of people paid it no mind.

The driver of the first car, a short balding man wearing a pinstriped suit and sunglasses, stepped to the front.

"Hey, are you two the owners of these bizarre things, or merely the owners' agents?"

When the twins didn't answer right away, he stamped his foot impatiently.

"Well, which is it? Speak up, I haven't got all day," he said.

"Owners, sir!" Ellen quickly said. "Each one of these magnificent creatures is from our own personal collection!"

"Well then, good! Good, good, good!" the balding man said. "Excellent! No need to dicker with a representative when you can do business with the owner face-to-face! Allow me to introduce myself."

The man reached inside his jacket and with one smooth, practised move, snapped out a small white card and presented it to Ellen. Edgar looked over her shoulder and they both read what was engraved on it in bold black type:

Mr Marvin Matterhorn
Executive Business Executive

When they looked up, every adult had pulled out his or her business card and was offering it to the twins impatiently. Edgar and Ellen collected them all, each one printed with the person's name and the title "Business Executive" or "Assistant Business Executive" or "Junior Business Executive."

"Well, we haven't got all day. We're carpooling to work," said Mr Matterhorn. "Very efficient, carpooling!"

The business people behind him murmured, "Very efficient, indeed!"

Mr Matterhorn removed his sunglasses and whipped a monogrammed *MM* handkerchief out of his pocket. As he cleaned the lenses, he continued:

"What we need are animals, pets for our kids who can't seem to stop their blasted crying. We were all up half the night searching high and low, trying to find the cats and dogs that ran away yesterday. And each and every one of us had a miserable night's sleep. Do you have *any* idea how lack of sleep affects our on-the-job performance?"

"Our performance, indeed!" agreed the others, nodding solemnly.

"Well, as I said, we need pets, and it certainly looks like the two of you have got them," Mr Matterhorn observed. "Although these creatures look rather peculiar."

"That's because they're exotic animals, sir," said Ellen. "Not anything like them in all the world!"

"Exotic? Is that right?" Mr Matterhorn replied. "Well, I know it's popular to have something that's 'one-of-a-kind,' but I prefer things to be as similar as possible. Easier to manage. Good management is everything. If something goes wrong, replace it with a duplicate and everything continues to run smoothly! Very efficient!"

"Very efficient, indeed!" chimed in his colleagues, who were now poking and prodding the strange little creatures.

Mr Matterhorn nodded. "Let's cut to the chase, shall we, and make a deal? This odd little critter would make my daughter Mandy forget all about her missing bunny rabbit," he said, examining a Boingabonga. "After all, bunnies don't have long yellow snouts and antennae like this thing. What is your asking price?"

"It's right there on the sign," Ellen pointed out. "Our price for a Boingabonga is $1,500."

"$1,500! Isn't that a bit steep?" exclaimed Mr Matterhorn.

"$1,500 is a steal! Our animals are exotic animals, and according to all the experts, *exotic* animals are *valuable* animals," Ellen responded.

"Besides, these animals are from our own personal collection," she said, trying to drum up sympathy. "We hate to part with our treasures, but we must, now that our poor family has fallen on such hard times."

Mr Matterhorn adjusted his sunglasses. "I'm sorry to hear you're in financial trouble. I make it my business to avoid that type of problem. But dealings like these require some negotiation, young lady. You can't expect us to hand over that kind of money for a *pet!* We just need something to keep our kids quiet. What do you say to – let me think for a moment – ten dollars?"

"Ten dollars?" repeated Ellen. "I say ten dollars is an awful lot less than fifteen hundred!"

"All right, then. Twenty."

Ellen shook her head and glared at Mr Matterhorn.

"You drive a hard bargain, miss, but you have to learn how to negotiate!" said the executive, beads of sweat forming on top of his hairless head. "You'll never get *anywhere* in business if you don't learn how to negotiate! Fifty dollars, and that's my final offer!"

Ellen faced the crowd, doing her best to seem taller than she was. "My brother and I are not here to negotiate, we're here to sell. These are valuable, exotic animals! And if you won't give us what they're worth, then you should leave!"

Mr Matterhorn looked annoyed. "To be quite frank, there is no way we are going to pay you *that* kind of money for any of these little monsters. I wouldn't be surprised if you didn't sell a single one.

"And this is an odd place for you to set up shop, isn't it? The people passing through here are going to work! And people who work as hard we do, do it to *make* money, not *spend* it. Don't forget the three rules of retail: Location! Location! Location!"

"Isn't that just one rule?" asked Edgar. "Repeated three times?"

"That's because it's so important, young man! You're lucky we're here at all!" bellowed Mr Matterhorn.

Ellen grimaced. "Well, you just don't realize what you're missing. Imagine, walking away from these delightful animals!"

Mr Marvin Matterhorn's mouth formed a hard line across his fleshy face. "Oh, we'll come out on top of this deal – we always do. I'll keep my eye out for you on our way home this evening. I'm sure you'll have dropped your ridiculous prices by then!"

"Ridiculous, indeed!" the chorus echoed.

Mr Matterhorn held his pose for several silent seconds as if to give Ellen one more chance to change her mind. Then with a loud "Humph!" he stomped back to his car.

The other business people followed, uttering a collective "Humph!" as they turned away from the

Exotic Animal Emporium and marched to their cars. Doors slammed shut, and the vehicles departed.

Ellen glowered as she watched them disappear down Ricketts Road. Then she noticed Edgar standing there, smirking.

"What are you smiling about, you dolt?" she fumed. "You didn't help me try to sell these things at all, and now we've lost all those customers!"

"Oh, stop your whining!" Edgar retorted. "Those pompous windbags are idiots.

"They don't pay attention to their own kids, so I figured, why would they pay attention to me? While you were dealing with them, I sneaked over to their cars and stuck tacks and nails in front of their wheels!

"They'll be stranded for hours! Think of all the business deals they'll miss!"

Ellen tugged on a pigtail and said, "Business, *indeed!*"

> *Mr Marvin Matterhorn*
> *Looks at us with so much scorn*
> *Cares not why his kid's forlorn –*
> *He's such a selfish dad!*
> *We know what it's like to be*

Abandoned to our roguery
Just wait until those kids come see
The pets they might have had!

17. Relocation

Edgar pointed at the cars passing by them. "Everyone around here seems to be concentrating very hard on getting where they are going."

Ellen nodded. "If no one will notice us here, let's keep moving."

So they continued on, Ellen struggling with the rusted handle to make the turn onto Rio Road.

"Blast it, Edgar, why didn't you oil these axles and hinges when we had the chance?"

"Well, why didn't *you?*" The twins made hideous faces at each other. Though it was a contest they often kept up for hours, they had a more important mission today. They turned their attention back to rolling the ungainly cart. Not far down the street they found a spot at the edge of a small park. While they were getting the display ready, they noticed some movement on Sydney Street, a short block away. Two small boys, a few years younger than the twins, were crawling out of a culvert beneath the road. The wide-mouthed metal pipe was used to drain water after thunderstorms so the street wouldn't flood, and the area around the culvert was often a swampy mess.

Crusty sludge and small bits of trash covered each boy from head to toe. It looked as if they had been crawling through culverts for some time now, and a thick coating of sewer slime made their hair colour and the patterns on their clothes unidentifiable. But the twins clearly saw their puffy red eyes and the tear streaks in the grime on their faces.

"Brother, aren't those the Turkle boys? Burl and Seth? I can't stand those little whiners!"

Edgar squinted, now recognizing the Turkles beneath the filth.

"Why, yes they are, Sister. I guess they can't find their pretty pooch. Serves them right!"

The twins watched as the two boys overturned rocks, picked through every small bush, and sorted through the trash littered about. After taking one last look into the culvert, the boys finally shrugged and trudged a short way up Sydney Street before disappearing inside another sewage pipe.

Edgar stood silent for a moment, staring after

them with envy. He took a deep breath and let out a long sigh.

"Ah, *sewers*. It's been a while since we've spent any quality time exploring them, Sister."

Ellen elbowed him in the ribs.

"There will be plenty of time to renew our acquaintance later, Brother. The sewers aren't going anywhere, you know, and we have work to do."

Edgar rubbed his side, sighed again, and turned back to the cart.

"Rare beasts for sale!" he bellowed.

18. Dairy Deliveries

While the morning sun was still low in the sky, a truck pulled up in front of the Exotic Animal Emporium, belching black smoke as it came to a stop. On the side of the truck was a peeling picture of a smiling cow eating a piece of Swiss cheese, with the words "Nod's Limbs Dairy" stencilled across the top.

A tall, powerfully built woman climbed down from the cab and looked at her rusty vehicle. Thick smoke poured out of its front and back ends.

"Aw, nuts," she said.

The twins watched her walk over to a pay phone at the corner of the park. She wore a clean white uniform with a black bow tie and a white cap. With her head held high and her chest puffed out, she looked like she was marching in a one-person military parade.

Either the person she was calling didn't answer, or the phone was out of order, for she suddenly slammed the phone back onto its cradle. She looked back at her truck and muttered something the twins couldn't hear.

Ellen loudly cleared her throat.

"Ahem."

Elsie Miller turned and looked surprised to see the twins and the elaborate cart full of creatures.

"Good morning, youngsters! What a beautiful day for you to be playing outside!

"And lookie here, aren't these just the *cutest* little things you've ever seen!" she said, approaching the particularly freakish Lollimop. The Lollimop bobbed its green polka-dotted head and clucked.

"But you two," she said as she leaned down close to the twins and pinched their ashen cheeks. "You look a little pale. You should drink more milk!"

Each sibling disliked being pinched by the other, so, needless to say, they both hated being pinched by someone else. Ellen was ready to give Elsie Miller a nasty pinch of her own when Edgar stomped on her foot and whispered, "Watch it! Don't drive away the customer!"

The dairy driver carefully studied the animals from top to bottom, sometimes lifting them off the table to inspect their undersides.

"Maybe you two can help me out," said Elsie as she checked under the tail of a bright orange Canterlamper. "I can't seem to find udders or nipples on any of these here critters. Everyone knows you can't make milk without udders or nipples! Down at the dairy, we've got plenty of cows, but we've found that goats make pretty good milk, too.

"Goats!" she continued. "Who would've thought? And I'm a milk connoisseur! If people like goat's milk and goat cheese, who's to say they won't like other kinds as well? I've got half a mind to start my own side business, selling milk and dairy products from other animals – it could be profitable. And I could get my own truck."

Elsie tugged doubtfully at a protrusion on the stomach of the Lollimop that looked remarkably like a bulb from a string of holiday lights. The Lollimop scratched at the cart uncertainly and clucked again.

"So…do any of these odd little critters make milk?"

Ellen scratched her forehead and said, "Milk? Sure! Some of them make milk. In fact, the most exotic of our animals produce the most delicious milk. That's why they're the most valuable!

"See that Mildewilder down there? Mmmm, *mmm!* And it's only *$3,000.* Think of all the exotic milk you could sell with your very own Mildewilder! You'd make back your investment in no time."

"Well, I think I'd like to sample some exotic Mildew-whatever milk! I wouldn't be a milk expert if I didn't try some, would I? But I'm sorry to say the Nod's Limbs Dairy can't afford $3,000, and I certainly can't afford it on my own. If the Dairy had that kind of cash, I'd make them fix my truck first! Just look at that heap of junk."

Elsie Miller glanced at the smoking vehicle and shook her head.

"Do any of your less expensive animals make milk?"

"Well, maybe the Mildewilder *is* a bit out of your league," Edgar sneered. "That's all right, I'm *sure* we could sell it to some *other* dairy who can appreciate the lucrative opportunity available with Mildewilder milk."

He pointed at a small, pink, feathered creature a bit farther down the line. "How about a Grobble? Its milk is not quite as refined as a Mildewilder's, but it is more affordable. Only $2,500!"

The dairy driver lifted her cap and ran her fingers

through her hair. "*Affordable?* Are you *serious?* Do you have something for maybe, say, $50?"

Edgar shuddered, realizing that neither the Nod's Limbs Dairy nor Elsie would make them rich.

"Our most inexpensive creatures are $1,000 and not a penny less, and we have no milk makers for under $2,000! So if you're not buying, please move your broken-down truck away from our emporium. That black smoke is scaring away all our customers and choking our animals."

Elsie shrugged and turned to leave when Ellen appeared with a glass full of cloudy liquid.

"Before you go, please try some of our splendid Mildewilder milk, on the house!" she said sweetly.

"Gosh," said Elsie as she took the glass, "that's very kind of you."

She swished the liquid around, sniffed it, and then held it up to the sunlight.

"It sure doesn't look very pure, but here goes!" She downed the liquid in one gulp.

"Hmmm," she said, savouring the taste on her tongue. "Very thin, not a lot of body for a good glass of milk. Not a whole lot of flavour, either. I guess it's just as well my dairy and I can't afford your animals, after all. They don't make very good milk."

With that, Elsie Miller climbed back into her rusty truck and drove off, explosive backfires of exhaust fading as she disappeared over a hill.

"Boy oh boy, that truck won't be the only thing backfiring soon!" said Ellen, snorting with laughter.

"What's so funny?" demanded Edgar. "We've just lost another customer and we *still* don't have any money! No money means no schemes! This is no laughing matter! And where the blazes did you get that milk, anyhow?"

"Oh, sourpuss, it wasn't *really* milk!" Ellen said once she caught her breath. "While you were dealing with Madame Milktruck, I got some laxative tablets out of your satchel – you know, the ones you took from Heimertz – and stirred them into a glass of water. They made plain water cloudy like milk, but it won't be long before she's making a mad dash to the bathroom! Hah!"

Edgar laughed, and the twins sang,

> *Elsie wants some milk that's clean*
> *But she drives that foul machine*
> *Coughing smoke – it's quite obscene –*
> *She'd better get that fixed!*
> *For us, a sale spilled down the drain*

While back at work she must explain
She feels a bit of tummy pain
From messing with our tricks!

19. On the Road

The twins finished their song and collapsed against each other, cackling and chortling. With a few last snickers, Ellen cast a fresh eye on their location.

"I don't think this spot is working either, Brother."

"Off again, I say." Edgar began to push the creaking wagon.

They pulled and pushed their way along Rio Road, across the edge of the Green Gables Community Golf Course, past pole after pole covered with "missing" and "lost" pet flyers. Finally, they stopped in front of the Nod's Limbs High School parking lot to rest.

School was closed for summer vacation, but there were some cars in the lot because the downtown shopping district was nearby.

Ellen stood in front of the cart, yelling "Rare BEASTS for sale!" while Edgar fiddled with the wagon's sticky wheels.

Suddenly, Ellen felt something pull on her leg.

Little Penny Pickens, so small that she barely reached Ellen's waist, looked up pleadingly, tugging at Ellen's striped pyjamas with her tiny hand. Ellen recognized the blonde five-year-old from the neighbourhood.

"'Scuse me, have you seen Mr Poo Poo?"

Ellen stared at Penny a moment.

"What in blazes is a Mr Poo Poo?"

Penny looked alarmed. "Didn't you see the signs my brother made? Ooh, you better be *careful!*"

Now she had the twins' ears. "Be careful" usually got their attention, since it often meant something unpleasant might happen.

"Whatever do you mean, little girl?" asked Edgar.

"Mr Poo Poo is gone! He's our pet snake and he got out! Big snakes can be very dangerous if you let them out. Mr Poo Poo wouldn't do anything to Peter or me – he's really nice and friendly – but some people don't know what to do around snakes!"

Edgar and Ellen grinned and poked each other.

"Oh wow, you should see him eat! Mr Poo Poo can open his mouth really, really wide, and he can swallow things that are bigger than his own head! It's *amazing!* And 'cause Mr Poo Poo is so big, the things he can eat are *huge!*

"He doesn't eat very often, but when he's hungry, you have to feed him right away. Then everything's okay, and he goes back to sleep. But if you don't feed him..."

Penny sighed and pointed toward the dumpsters near the school, where two kids were rummaging about, throwing papers and cans in the air. "All the other kids' pets disappeared last night, too! Those poor little animals! Everybody says they're just lost, but if Mr Poo Poo found them, maybe he ate them for dinner!"

Edgar and Ellen looked down at Penny, absolutely thrilled. Edgar cracked his knuckles in secret satisfaction, and Ellen bit her tongue to keep from smiling *too* broadly.

"I don't know what to do! We put signs all over town. Peter and I went to the fire department 'cause they can rescue cats from trees. They said they would tell everybody to look out for Mr Poo Poo. They just *have* to find him!"

As Penny Pickens sniffled, she finally caught sight of the elaborate cart, the animals still hidden behind the curtain.

"What's *that?* What does that sign say?"

Ellen leaned down and said, "Our sign says *'Special Jail for Little Girls.'* Now, scram before we throw you in!"

With a tiny yelp, Penny stepped back, staring first at Ellen, then Edgar, and then fled down the street, her final warning of "Look out for Mr Poo Poo!" hanging in the warm summer air.

"Well, I'm glad to get *her* out of our hair," Ellen said. "Who'd be afraid of that snake? All he does is sleep, and he's got a leash on him. Silly little girl."

20. Handle with Care

Edgar and Ellen took a moment to eat their lunch, a simple meal of dry salt crackers with olive paste and raisins. The exotic beasts watched them with hungry eyes, and when the Crackermacker tried to snatch a saltine from Ellen, she shooed it away. The twins had just finished eating when Mr Crapple, the mailman, neared.

As he reached Edgar and Ellen's mobile menagerie, he let his mailbag slide to the ground, placed his hands on his hips, and leaned backwards as far as

he could, arching his back until the twins heard a loud *"Crack!"*

"That's a little better," grumbled Mr Crapple. "Gosh darn aching back. Got to get Mrs Crapple to walk on it again tonight."

He glanced at the sign posted on the cart.

"Rare beasts, eh?"

Mr Crapple had been the mail carrier for Zone 13 of the Nod's Limbs Post Office for decades.

"Well, I hope you're not expecting to mail any of these creatures," growled Mr Crapple. "You'll need a special permit to send live animals. And you have to take them to the post office yourself. I don't carry permits on my route."

"We don't want to mail them," said Edgar. "We just want to sell them. It's our exotic animal collection."

"Exotic, eh?" said Mr Crapple. "What do you children know about exotic? All you dirty little ragamuffins, thinking you know everything. I doubt you've ever been outside dear sweet Nod's Limbs in your entire young lives! Not a thing wrong with Nod's Limbs, mind you, but a far cry from exotic!"

The mailman glared down at them. "You think *you* know exotic? *I* know exotic! I've served the Postmaster General for going on forty years and I've seen a little something from everywhere. I've hauled boxes from Borneo and packages from Paraguay! Delivered letters from Latvia and crates from the Congo! I've carried cartons from Canada and postcards from Pago Pago – held them right here in my very own hands! Don't tell *me* I don't know exotic when I see it!"

Mr Crapple lumbered up to the long wagon full of animals and looked them over. He squinted sceptically as he read the signs describing the animals.

"That's an awful lot of strange critters you have there, young-uns," acknowledged Mr Crapple as he reached Edgar and Ellen at the end of the cart. "Very unusual. But *exotic?* I don't know about that.

"Did any of them come from some faraway land overseas? That's the real sign of something exotic – if it came in the mail with colourful stamps all over it. Well, did they?"

Before Ellen could respond, the mailman said, "Of *course* they didn't come in the mail! If they had, I would have known about it!

"Hey, what's your strange little friend doing over there?" Mr Crapple pointed at Edgar, who was gathering rocks by the side of the road.

"Oh, don't mind him," said Ellen, rolling her eyes. "He's a bit off. Now, can I interest you in one of our amazing animals?

"Our Multipeeder is considered a worker of miracles in Plutavia. It has lots of little legs, and a little foot at the end of every one." Ellen held up the

brown and yellow creature, which was really a fat gerbil with several doll limbs glued to its body.

Returning to the cart, Edgar added, "This rare beast has quite a remarkable history. It was originally captured in the wild savannas of Rimpledop Province in south central Frinquay. We obtained it from a famous travelling musician – a harmonica player, the owner of the world's largest harmonica, in fact – who had back problems caused by carrying his heavy instrument case all over the world. Imagine how it would feel to have this cute little creature walk up and down your back! So many more feet than Mrs Crapple!"

Mr Crapple laughed dryly. "Listen, boy, my wife may have bumpy, smelly feet, but that critter you're holding looks like a giant hairy spider! There's no way on this great green earth that I'll let a nasty thing like that touch any part of me!"

Ellen scowled.

"I've wasted enough of my time," the postman continued, ignoring her, "I just needed to stretch my back before continuing my route. Here I am talking to you, and you don't even have any mail!"

"Pardon me sir, but I do have something to send," called out Edgar from the other end of the wagon. He pointed to a large package sitting on the ground.

"Where did that come from? Well, never mind then, don't dawdle. Put it in my mailbag over there," said Mr Crapple.

Edgar heaved the parcel into the mailbag. The new addition landed with a heavy thud.

Mr Crapple hoisted his mailbag over his shoulder, his eyes bulging and his knees buckling from the weight of it.

"Gee, how'd this thing get so heavy all of a sudden?" grunted Mr Crapple as he staggered down the street.

Edgar pulled one of Ellen's pigtails to get her attention. "This will be fun to see – I opened up one of his boxes and filled it with rocks!"

The twins watched as Mr Crapple hunched forwards and balanced the bag across his back, leaving his legs to shiver and shake under the heavy weight. The postman staggered to the left and staggered to the right and staggered every which way. With every lurch punctuated by a sharp cracking sound from his back, he slowly disappeared out of sight.

Snickering, Edgar and Ellen broke into song.

That mailman has a lot of gall
He really thinks he knows it all
But now his mailbag's hard to haul:
He made a big mistake.
A Multipeeder's what he lacks –
The thing to soothe those painful cracks
But he declined and now his back's
About to truly ache!

21. Rare Beast Expertise

"We are having absolutely NO luck," said Ellen, "I can't believe you've picked such awful places to set up our cart!"

"*I* picked? You're the one steering this contraption!"

Ellen ignored her brother's retort and lifted the cart's handle.

"Come on, Edgar, it's still just early afternoon. Maybe we can find some suckers, I mean *customers,* closer to the river."

So the twins pushed past Greasy Billy's Gas Station, turned onto Florence Boulevard, and set up shop near the public library. From where they stood, they were within sight of one of the seven covered bridges in town, the one with "TAKE" on one side of the roof, and "FRIEND" on the other.

Soon, a white-maned gentleman bounded up the road. Large round spectacles perched atop his nose, and his lab coat flapped as he moved like the wings of an agitated goose. He was looking every which way, up and down and around, clearly searching for something. The wiry man was so intent on looking everywhere except where he was going that he almost crashed right into the Exotic Animal Emporium.

"HEY!" yelled Edgar and Ellen.

Startled, the man stopped.

"Oh my! Very sorry!" he said, "Have the two of you seen anything odd today? Any strange slithering movements near the ground? I'm looking for an escaped python. The fire department contacted me because I'm an animal expert. Firefighters may be very capable at rescuing cats from trees, but tracking pythons is a bit out of their league! But fear not, I'll find it."

He paused as he looked past the twins, focusing on the "Rare Beasts" sign and then on the long stage cluttered with creatures.

"Oh, my."

He dashed up to the closest creature, a green-and-orange-tinted Jollypoddle, and quickly examined it.

"Oh, my!"

He eyeballed the next exotic pet, a large feathered thing with long scraggly teeth called a Windelstump.

"Oh, my!" he said once more, his eyes widening behind the thick glasses.

The animated gentleman skipped along the length of the cart, briefly examining each creature as he went. And with every new discovery, he flailed his arms about in the air or kicked his legs out in a jig or jumped up and down in fits of laughter.

"Oh, *MY!*"

Edgar and Ellen stood speechless, startled by his obvious enthusiasm. He hurried up to them, standing so close that they could read the laminated badge clipped to his lab coat:

DR FELIX VON BARLOW
Senior Zoologist
Nod's Limbs Zoo

On the right side was a close-up photo of Dr Von Barlow, his mouth open and his eyes bulging.

Ellen suppressed a laugh.

Edgar said, "Zoologist?"

"No, young man. A 'zo-ologist.' There's no such thing as a 'zoo-ologist.' People always mispronounce my profession. And I'm a *senior* zoologist, actually, in charge of all the animals at the Nod's Limbs Zoo. Nothing happens there without my say so," said Dr Von Barlow. "Tell me, have you two little ones been there? Children just adore the zoo."

Edgar and Ellen had indeed been to the zoo on several occasions, once, in fact, to "borrow" a few piranhas from the fish tank to put in a kiddie pool. The zoo didn't have much else that interested them. It was basically a large petting zoo, with common animals like cows and pigs and goats. There was a reindeer one winter, brought in especially for the holiday season. The only real fun the twins ever had there was when they scared a group of skunks into spraying the Gribble family. It had made quite a dent in the Gribbles' social life.

"We don't like your zoo," said Ellen. "You don't have any interesting attractions."

Dr Von Barlow's happy mood vanished, and he let out a deep sigh.

"Oh, you're right, you're *right,*" he lamented. "Here I am, having spent my whole life studying and learning everything there is to know about every different kind of animal, and look at me! I hurry, hurry, *hurry* myself to work every day, so I can spend my time making sure the pigs' tails stay curly and the cows don't catch colds.

"I spent years and years at university, getting various degrees that should have made me an international star of zoology, with a life full of exciting world travel and impressive speaking engagements. *I* should have my own television show on the global satellite station Planète Animale, not that nitwit Professor Paul.

"I tell the zoo's board of directors, 'Let's get a seal,' or 'How about a lion?' or 'Kids love pandas.' All they say is, 'What's wrong with squirrels?' and 'Sheep are nice.' About the only interesting thing we have these days is our colony of fire ants! Actually, I was in the middle of some scientific examinations when the fire department called, so I had to bring some specimens with me."

The zoologist withdrew a sealed glass jar from the folds of his lab coat and set it down on the edge of the wagon. The twins peered closely at the little red insects milling about inside.

Von Barlow paused, lost in thought. Edgar was lost in a thought of his own, entranced by the fire ants.

"Sister, owners' conference," whispered Edgar as he pulled Ellen aside. "I want those fire ants. Maybe we can trade him!"

Ellen twisted Edgar's ear. "Oh, I know you, Brother. You'd have lots of ideas for what *we* could do with nasty, biting fire ants, but at the first chance you'd dump them under *my* bedcovers! Well, I'll have none of that."

With one last twist, Ellen let go of her brother's ear and turned back to Von Barlow.

"Maybe we have exactly what you need, Doctor."

His face lit up. "Oh yes, you very well may! I just can't believe all the fabulous animals you have here! This may be the greatest day of my career!"

Edgar and Ellen smirked and kicked at each other.

"So you might be interested in some of our rare, exotic creatures?" Ellen asked.

"Interested?" the zoologist replied. "Why I'm downright *obsessed* with these fantastic creatures! Just *look* at them! I've seen all kinds of beasts, but I have never, I repeat, *never,* come across anything like these! All new species! Never seen before! However did you get them? Oh, never mind how you got them! They're incredible!"

"They are?" said Edgar.

"Of course they are! These animals will make me famous! The board of directors will erect a huge new building at the zoo! The Von Barlow Hall of Rare and Exotic Species! Zoologists from all over the world will come to see them, and they'll say 'That Von Barlow, he's the best there is!' *Von Barlow Is Our Hero,* I can see the headlines now! I'll be promoted to Executive Zookeeper, awarded honorary degrees and titles..."

He could barely contain himself, giggling and dancing and skipping in front of the cart.

"Well, Dr Von Barlow, which of our amazing species would you like?" asked Ellen, eager to finally make her first sale.

"Which?" retorted the zoologist. "*Which?* Why, I don't want some of these creatures, I want all of them!"

"You want...*all of them?*" the twins repeated.

"Every last one!" boomed Von Barlow, picking up a dazed Fuddleflinger and giving it a great big hug. But as he swung the Fuddleflinger about, the muzzle on its snout loosened and fell off, and everyone froze as it let out a halfhearted "Woof."

"Oh, my!" said the zoologist, "That sounded...just like..."

Edgar and Ellen glanced at each other. All their hard work would be for naught if Dr Von Barlow

figured out that the Fuddleflinger was just a beagle puppy in disguise.

The zoologist stammered, "...just like...like a... *Troeuilompe!* That's it! Have you ever heard of one? I always have a hard time with French pronunciation. I was fortunate enough to receive a recording of its wild call through my membership in the Animal-of-the-Month Club. I wonder if the Fuddleflinger species is related."

He laughed, and playfully woofed along with the animal.

Relieved, Edgar displayed his happiest expression, which, coincidentally, was also his creepiest. Things were going well.

Ellen sauntered down the side of the cart, adding up the value of each exotic animal.

"Well, Dr Von Barlow," she said, "we have a great many rare beasts here, and you know that *rare* means *valuable*. But since you're willing to keep the collection together – and we'll miss them so, the adorable little things – I'm sure we can make some concessions."

She scratched her chin, pulled on her pigtails, and said "hmm" a lot as she mulled things over.

"I'm sure you'll agree, Doctor, that for all of these magnificent creatures, a nice round figure of $25,000 is a generous selling price."

The Fuddleflinger yelped as Dr Von Barlow dropped it to the ground.

"*Sell? $25,000?* Oh, no, my dear! No, no, *no!* I'm afraid you just don't understand! Nod's Limbs Zoo is a public zoo. You don't *sell* animals to us, you *donate* them!"

"*Donate?!*" howled Edgar. "You mean, give them to you for *no money?* Why would we want to do that?"

"Why?" said Von Barlow. "Well, you will get a nice plaque on the wall at the zoo!"

"We get our names on a *plaque?!*" said Ellen. "Let me get this straight – we give you our animals for free, and you get famous and get your name in journals and get a *building* dedicated to you, and all we get is a measly *plaque?*"

"Well, yes!" said the zoologist. "You should see them. They're really quite lovely. Very nicely engraved!"

Dr Von Barlow picked up the Fuddleflinger and reaffixed its muzzle. While Edgar's pasty complexion was turning an angry red at the prospect of another lost sale, Ellen grabbed a mallet from the depths of her brother's satchel and raised it up over her head.

The twins faced each other, Ellen swinging the mallet madly and both hopping from foot to foot. Slightly beyond earshot of Von Barlow, in hushed voices they chanted:

> *Von Barlow thinks he knows his stuff*
> *We two are here to call his bluff*
> *These animals are rare enough*
> *To make his reputation.*
> *But we won't give these beasts away*
> *If he wants fame he'll have to pay*
> *We're through with cheapskates for today*
> *Here comes some compensation!*

The zoologist was lucky, because as Ellen readied her swing, a flashy red fire truck with a big gold "7" painted on the door pulled up in front of their wagon.

22. Lucky Engine Number 7

"What's all this?" shouted one of the firefighters hanging on the back of the truck.

"Oh, it's a fantastic collection of rare and exotic

animals," said Dr Von Barlow, looking up, "Absolutely inspiring…"

"Well now, Doctor, have you found the python?" called out the driver.

"Oh, yes, the python," the zoologist said. "I'd rather forgotten about *that*…"

The firefighters climbed off the truck. One of them tilted her helmet back and said, "We haven't had much luck on the snake hunt, either. Lucky Engine Number 7 isn't too lucky today."

"Dreadful," muttered Von Barlow.

"Yeah, Doc, we're starting to get worried. Having that snake on the loose, well, that's *bad*. All those poor kids, you really feel for 'em, you know? Their little pets, stuffed down in some huge, slimy reptile's belly."

Edgar and Ellen listened with interest.

"Things could get *real* sticky. Word has leaked to the press about this snake situation, and you know those reporters when it comes to something like this! It'll be all over the headlines by tonight. We could have a full-scale panic on our hands!"

The twins whispered to one another.

"Did you hear that, Brother? A panic! That means everyone will be running and screaming in the streets, right?"

"The whole town, Sister! The whole town will be in a snit! I think that might be a record for us!"

Just then Sparkplug, the dalmatian mascot for Lucky Engine Number 7, leapt down from the truck and bounded toward the cart. Edgar and Ellen watched with horror as the firehouse dog nosed around the animals, sniffing and grunting and slobbering. Disturbed, the beasts began to strain against their leashes.

"No!" yelled the twins, leaping at Sparkplug.

Ellen grabbed the dog's collar, trying to pull her head back. Edgar wrapped his arms around the dog's body to drag her away from the cart. But Sparkplug was big and strong, and the twins didn't have much success. Fortunately, the dog got a noseful of glitter, which made her sneeze loudly and uncontrollably.

"Sparkplug!"

A firefighter called the dog, who dropped her head and slunk back to the truck, letting loose a few glittery sneezes as she went.

Edgar sighed in relief, but just as Ellen was launching into a sales pitch to convince the fire department to purchase a more exotic mascot, a fleet of bicycles appeared, speeding down Florence Boulevard.

23. The Search Party

Suddenly, the area around the Exotic Animal Emporium became very crowded as a pack of neighbourhood children pulled up.

With eyes red and puffy from hours of crying, two dozen children looked up pleadingly at the firefighters and the zoologist. Occasionally a sniffle could be heard from the back of the group.

"Have you found them yet? Have you found our pets?" asked Willa Malloy, whose green bike was at the front of the pack.

Little Annie Krump covered her face with her hands and muffled a sob. Willa cast a sympathetic look over her shoulder.

"I'm sorry, young lady," said a firefighter, "but we haven't found a trace of them. We may have to accept the worst."

"*No!* We don't believe our pets were eaten! Not *all* of them, they couldn't have been!"

"Now, kids, I know it's hard..." said the firefighter.

"Well, did you find the snake? Was its stomach huge?" asked Willa.

"Uh, no, we haven't located the snake yet," Von Barlow admitted, "but we'll catch it soon!"

Willa hung her head between her handlebars for a moment and then straightened up again. "You expect us to believe that all our pets just up and ran away, or that some huge snake ate every single one of them? That's crazy!"

The firefighters and Dr Von Barlow looked away, unable to think of anything that could possibly console the children.

But Edgar and Ellen thought of something to say.

"We're very sorry to hear about your misfortunes, but maybe a sweet new pet is just what you need to take your minds off your losses," said Edgar.

"We happen to have some very nice exotic pets for sale right here," said Ellen.

The twins smiled, doing their best to appear sympathetic. Willa swung off her bike and let it fall with a clatter. She snapped at them, pointing her finger accusingly. "What makes you think we'd want *new* pets? And why would we want them from the two of you? We remember the mean tricks you've played on us!"

"Yeah!" yelled some of the other children.

"Our animals are out there somewhere, trying to find their way back to us, I just know it! We've been searching all day, and we're not going to give up now!" Willa pointed to a young girl covered in puffy red welts, "Heather searched the edge of the Black Tree Forest, and all she found were hundreds of mosquitoes.

"Seth and Burl Turkle spent the morning looking in disgusting sewer pipes..."

Edgar and Ellen recognized the two boys from earlier that day, still covered head to toe with slime and glop.

"...they smell so bad, we made them ride in the back.

"Amy, Frannie, and Ronnie turned up nothing in

the alley behind the school – well, except for a few fat rats, but who likes *rats?*"

At the mention of rats, Edgar nodded at his sister. They'd had some fun times with rats.

"Leanne and Bruno didn't have any luck at the construction sites, and Sondra looked under every car and truck in town."

Willa let out a sigh of despair, and the children behind her made little choked-up sounds.

The tall girl leaned toward the twins and waved a finger under their noses. "We're not going to let you two pull anything on us."

"Pull something on you?" said Ellen sweetly. "Why – we'd never! Why don't you just take a peek at what we've got. No pressure to buy, of course..." She trailed off and took a step back to reveal the rare beasts.

Willa resisted for a moment, but curiosity won out and she reluctantly approached the wagon. The rest of the children parked their bicycles and followed her.

Muzzled, the exotic beasts purred and whined desperately, but their beloved owners didn't recognize them. The animals strained against their leashes and hopped in place, all except for the lethargic

Mondopillar, who napped
in the back.

"Hey, look at this,"
squealed Carolyn South as
she squeezed the bulbous
nose of a crusty yellow
Guttlebug. *"Gross!"*

Calvin Hucklebee lift-
ed up the rubbery
forked tail of a
Shump and whis-
tled. *"Freaky!"*

Willa rapped her
knuckles against the hard, shiny head of a Hootlet,
and the metallic clang made her wonder aloud,
"What is this thing's skull made out of?"

"Do NOT touch the animals! They need their
rest – some of them are jet-lagged from their jour-
neys." Ellen pushed back the kids who were poking
and prodding the valuable items.

"If each one of you takes home one of these rare
exotic creatures," she added, "it won't be long before
you forget all about your old, plain pets. You'll be
the proud owners of the most unique animals in
the world!"

"But we don't *want* to forget about our pets!" cried Annie.

"They're part of our *families!*" wailed Seth.

"And who wants exotic animals when they're creepy and ugly and weird?" asked Willa. "How can I curl up in bed with *this* one?" she continued, pointing at a Lompa. "Those pointy horns would scratch me all night. Anyway, we're kids! Sondra's paper route, Burl and Seth's lawnmower service, and all of our allowances together couldn't buy a single one of these things, even if we wanted them. Your prices are *outrageous.*"

Edgar and Ellen stared at each other. Their hands curled into fists.

24. Fuel to the Fire

A loud screech of tyres made everyone turn around. Car doors slammed, and Marvin Matterhorn and his fellow executives stormed up to the firefighters.

"What's the meaning of *this?*" he spat, holding up a newspaper and jabbing his finger at the front page.

It was a special evening edition of the *Nod's Limbs Gazette*. The headline screamed:

"*First,* we're up all night tending to our crying kids! *Then* we had to spend all day changing flat tyres! And *now,* you're creating a panic by telling us something might eat our kids? This is *unacceptable!*"

"Unacceptable, indeed!" piped up the other business people. Many of them had stained shirts and dirty knees.

Mr Matterhorn was about to unleash further insults about the fire department's incompetence when he caught sight of Edgar and Ellen.

"Oh, it's you two," he said crossly. "Have you lowered your prices yet? That ten dollars is still burning a hole in my pocket!"

And that sent the twins over the edge.

25. Edgar and Ellen Face Off

"No one has any money!" screeched Edgar.

"Everybody wants us to just *give* these things away!" said Ellen.

"How are we going to do everything we want to do?!" they yelled at each other. *"It's all YOUR fault!"*

"MY fault?"

"ARRGH!"

The twins stood nose to nose in the midst of a crowd silenced by their sudden outburst. The adults were taken aback by the siblings' ferocity. The other children weren't surprised by it at all.

"I can't *believe* we haven't made *one single sale* all dreary day! Where are our riches? Where are our buckets of money?" said Edgar.

"*Our* riches? *Our* money? Forget *our!* Where's *mine?* I should get a reward for putting up with you and your stupid schemes!" Ellen yelled back.

"Oh, you selfish little snot!" Edgar sneered, raising himself up on tiptoe. "It's always you, you, *you!* If your sales skills weren't so *pathetic*, we'd have enough cash to do absolutely anything we want to do, right now!"

Ellen leaned toward Edgar threateningly.

"*My* skills! You buffoon! You mess up *everything!*" she retorted, strings of spittle flying through the air between them.

"Oh *yeah?*" shouted Edgar as he stomped on Ellen's foot.

"*Yeah!*" hollered Ellen as she reared back and kicked Edgar in the shin.

The children encircled the fray, watching the whole exchange, and they yelled out, "It's a *FIGHT!*"

The twins, hopping around in pain, started pulling each other's hair.

"*Fight! Fight! Fight!*" the children chanted, and the adults craned their necks for a better view.

Ellen swung her arms around and boxed her brother's ears. Edgar howled.

"*Fight! Fight! Fight!*"

Edgar pinched his sister's nose between his knuckles, then knocked the wind out of her with a knee to the stomach.

"*Fight! Fight! Fight!*"

Ellen rushed at Edgar, and Edgar rushed at Ellen, and they tackled each other in front of the Exotic Animal Emporium, crashing to the ground and rolling about in the dirt.

"*Fight! Fight! Fight!*" the crowd continued, unable

to tell the combatants apart in their dirty striped pyjamas.

The din of battle and the roar of the crowd grew louder and louder, and at long last Mr Poo Poo awoke from his slumber.

He was hungry.

26. Snakes Will Be Snakes

Many people keep puppies and kitties as pets, and it's easy to see why. Puppies and kitties are cute. They cock their little heads and look up at you with their loving eyes, and they're faithful and loyal and always happy to see you. They like to rub up against your legs and curl up in your lap, lick your hand and get you to stroke their fur. But not everybody keeps puppies and kitties for pets.

Some people, like Peter and Penny Pickens, keep Burmese pythons.

And as their owners know, a Burmese python can grow to be over twenty feet long and as thick as a tree trunk. A snake doesn't look at you with loving eyes because it has snake eyes and snake eyes always look like they're up to something. And a snake doesn't have fur for you to stroke, so if it curls up against you, it's probably hungry and thinks you'll make a tasty meal.

The twins had never owned a Burmese python themselves, so they knew nothing about the natural tendencies of a giant snake. They had merely snatched the Pickens' python as they had snatched all the other pets in the neighbourhood and disguised it as a great multicoloured Mondopillar, an especially exotic animal with a pointed snout, curling antennae, and feathers down the length of its limbless body.

Since everyone was fixated on the fight, no one remained around the Exotic Animal Emporium to notice the hungry Mondopillar make its move. Its flexibility made it inevitable that the Mondopillar would eventually wriggle out of its bonds. Slowly, it began to move down the length of the cart, smelling delicious things with its tongue.

The other animals were still leashed in place, and from the Mondopillar's perspective, all the puppies and kitties and bunnies were laid out like an all-you-can-eat buffet. The giant snake slithered forward, and the helpless little creatures in its path could do nothing to save themselves.

The Mondopillar first reached the miniature

Hamble, the itty-bitty kitty painted three shades of purple with a shiny red nose and pointy antlers on its head. The Mondopillar opened its great jaws wide and swallowed the Hamble in one big gulp, continuing toward the roly-poly feathered hamster the twins had named a Druffle.

Then, just as the oversized eating machine was about to inhale a second savoury morsel, the Mondopillar froze in its track.

27. An Attention Getter

The Hamble's antlers had caught in the Mondopillar's throat. All kinds of loud, nasty wheezes and coughs came from the python as it choked and gagged.

Now, Edgar and Ellen were yelling at the top of their lungs as they fought, and the roar of the surrounding crowd was very loud indeed, but the vile sounds made by the distressed snake were even louder. Everyone turned to see the source of the fearsome racket, the fight temporarily forgotten.

As the crowd watched, the Mondopillar coiled its body, raising itself high in the air and thrashing wildly about. Its head swayed from side to side and then reared back, and suddenly, with one tremendous *"grrahhkk!"* the snake dislodged the Hamble trapped in its throat.

Tufts of purple fur, a round, red ball and splinters from what had been antlers arched through the air in a spray of snake spittle, followed by a slimy kitty with mismatched eyes that looked awfully glad to be outside of the python.

"Chauncey!" screamed Donald Bogginer when he recognized his pet. Donald picked up the kitty and hugged him tightly.

"These aren't valuable exotic animals! They're our pets!"

28. No One Likes a Bath

The children swarmed over Engine Number 7. They grabbed water hoses and sprayed the cart and its contents from top to bottom. All the dyes, paints, and decorations washed away, and an exuberant cheer erupted from the crowd as the animals were revealed. The boys and girls were thrilled to see their pets, but not as happy as their pets were to see them!

While some of the children ran to the cart, a few remained on the truck. They increased the water pressure and took aim at the causes of their misery.

The water hit the twins full on.

"Glug!" yelped Edgar.

"Blarp!" gargled Ellen.

The blast knocked the pair completely off their feet, and turned the ground beneath them into a swampy mess.

One by one, the children gathered up their pets from the table, laughing and cuddling as the animals licked and nuzzled them. And one by one, they stomped past Edgar and Ellen, who wallowed helplessly in the mud pit.

"This is for Freckles!" said Stanley Mulligan, thumbing his nose.

"And *this* is for Blumpers!" said little Annie Krump, yanking Ellen's pigtail as she splashed by.

"And *this* is for our Mr Poo Poo!" declared Peter Pickens, kicking mud as he marched past carrying the tail end of the reptile. Penny, holding its front end, paused a moment as if to consider allowing the snake to make a meal of its captors. As the Pickens children carried their pet away, Mr Poo Poo stuck his long, slithering tongue out at the twins.

And to make matters even more miserable, Von Barlow's jar of fire ants had shattered in the chaos. They scurried through the slop and all over Edgar and Ellen, taking tiny, painful chomps out of them as they went.

"*Ow!*" Edgar yelped at each bite.

"You and your stupid fire ants!" cried Ellen, slapping herself in a fruitless effort to combat the insects. "Are you happy now? *Ouch!*"

After every child reclaimed his or her pet, after every child tromped past the mud-soaked twins, some with their executive parents in tow, after the firefighters rolled up their fire hose and drove Lucky Engine Number 7 out of sight, and after the crestfallen Dr Felix Von Barlow wandered away down the street, Edgar and Ellen were left alone with the ants in the cold, foul mud.

29. Close of Business

Covered with bruises, scratches, and bites, and dripping with oozing filth and mangled holiday decorations, Edgar and Ellen trudged back home and through the front door without bothering to wipe their feet. They didn't wipe their hands, arms, or legs, either, so as they slunk through the dank house they left trails of mud and dirty glitter in their wake.

"We sure learned a valuable lesson today, Brother," said Ellen, yawning.

"You're right, Sister," said Edgar. "The next time we disguise a bunch of stolen animals, we'll make sure not to use water-based paints and cheap glue — that stuff washes right off!"

Exhausted, Edgar and Ellen slowly climbed the dark stairs. Halfway up the third flight, an eerie feeling crept over them. They turned and there, cloaked in the shadows of the stairwell, Heimertz stood silently, his toothy smile flashing in the darkness. The twins scurried up the steps.

Near the top, they passed the den where Pet was again perched atop the wingback chair, intently watching a rerun of the very same nature show that had given them the idea for the Exotic Animal Em-porium

in the first place. One glance at the programme caused Edgar and Ellen to grimace and look away.

"*Arrgh,* animals! I *hate* animals, they're more trouble than they're worth!" moaned Ellen. "If we never ever see another puppy, kitty, bunny, or hamster, it'll be too soon!"

"And don't forget giant Burmese pythons," said Edgar, "or rather, DO forget giant Burmese pythons!"

One last song escaped from them as they slunk along, with all the glee of a funeral dirge:

> *Our plans, our scams – for naught we sought*
> *Exotic beasts that no one bought.*
> *A wasted day – we still have not*
> *A dime to spend on future plots.*
> *But all those goody-goodies will*
> *Soon find themselves more miserable*
> *When we return with coffers full*
> *And schemes more diabolical.*
> *Just wait, just wait, for back we'll be*
> *To cause more pain and misery.*

With that, the twins marched past the den, up the stairs and through the trapdoor to bed, leaving a filthy trail of footprints and handprints behind them.

30. The End of the Broadcast Day

Pet was left alone in the den, the light from the television casting deep shadows in the dark room. Once again, Edgar and Ellen hadn't stayed long enough to hear Professor Paul's final words on exotic animals:

> *"This odd creature is possibly the rarest animal on the planet, and sightings of the elusive beast are few and far between. It is not known for sure how many still live out there in the wild, and this scarcity makes them easily the most valuable exotic animals in the world."*

On the snowy black-and-white screen, the camera zoomed in on a tattered page from an old zoology book, showcasing a creature that looked very much like a dark, matted, greasy hairball with one yellowish eye.

Pet descended from the chair. Its dark, matted, greasy hairball of a body shambled off to bed, its single yellowish eye casting a faint glow as it disappeared into the shadows.

THE END

Edgar & Ellen

TOURIST TRAP

IT'S ELECTION SEASON IN NOD'S LIMBS, and Edgar and Ellen get wind of plans for an initiative to boost the local economy. The town's pending landmark status and the Mayor's own reputation depend on making Nod's Limbs a premier tourist destination. Edgar and Ellen will make sure the goody-goody Mayor and townspeople get all the attention they deserve!

If you're feeling brave, visit
Edgar and Ellen at:

www.EdgarAndEllen.com

Oh, the horror!

What people are saying about

Edgar & Ellen
and
RARE BEASTS

'RARE BEASTS was a great book. I loved this book because it was exciting and suspenseful. I had fun reading it and could not put it down. I can't wait for the next book. Hurry, Charles Ogden!'

—Jack F, age 10

'Edgar and Ellen are SO bad . . . I love them.'

—Conor, age 12

'I hope there are more Edgar and Ellen books because [RARE BEASTS is] really good.'

—Noah, age 8

Coming soon in the Edgar & Ellen series!

Book 2: Tourist Trap

Book 3: Under Town

Book 4: Pet's Revenge

Book 5: High Wire

Book 6: Nod's Limbs

Edgar & Ellen

UNDER TOWN

SOMEONE IS CAUSING a lot of trouble in the charming town of Nod's Limbs, but it isn't Edgar and Ellen! To catch this new mischievous miscreant and end the rash of copycat capers, the twins must scour the sewers and uncover someone's dirty secret.

Coming Soon!

WWW.EDGARANDELLEN.COM